Saying Grace
A Prayer of Thanksgiving

Written by Virginia Kroll
Illustrated by Timothy Ladwig

ZONDERVAN.com/
AUTHORTRACKER
follow your favorite authors

With love to Pat Rooney,
Patricia Harris, and Patricia Ahrens,
a trio of prayerful friends.
—V.K.

For the Claassen, Hall, and Landis families
who provided inspiration for painting.
My warmest thanks to you all.
—T.L.

Saying Grace
Copyright © 2009 by Virgina Kroll
Illustrations © 2009 by Timothy Ladwig

Requests for information should be addressed to: Zonderkidz, *Grand Rapids, Michigan 49530*

Zonderkidz, *Grand Rapids, Michigan 49530*

Library of Congress Cataloging-in-Publication Data
Kroll, Virgina L.
   Saying Grace: a prayer of thanksgiving / written by Virginia Kroll.
      p. cm. -- (Traditions of faith)
   Summary: Grace is worried about the coming winter, but happily it proves to be mild, and the next fall when Thanksgiving is celebrated, she starts a tradition of giving blessings to God before the meal. Includes author's note about the history of saying grace.
   ISBN-13: 978-0-310-71210-7 (hardcover : alk. paper)
   [1. Grace at meals--Fiction. 2. Thanksgiving Day--Fiction.] I. Title.
   PZ7.K9227Gr 2009
   [E]--dc22

                                                                                    2007013705

Editor: Amy DeVries
Art direction and design: Sarah Molegraaf

Printed in China

09 10 11 12 • 6 5 4 3 2 1

Do not be anxious about anything, but in everything, by prayer and petition, with thanksgiving, present your requests to God.

—Philippians 4:6

AUTHOR'S NOTE

There is no official biblical law or teaching in the church that instructs us to say grace before (and sometimes after) meals. Yet the custom was widely practiced as early as biblical times, not only by Christians, but by people in other cultures and religions as well. Chinese people, Native Americans, Jewish people, Buddhists, Muslims, Mormons, and Hindus all have special prayers to thank God for their food and to bless it.

Where did this tradition come from? The practice might have started in North America during the 1600s with an early settler like the girl in my fictional story. Grace realizes she should raise her voice in thanksgiving for the blessings God pours out over her, her family, and her friends.

Some anonymously written Christian mealtime prayers that have been passed on for generations include the following:

> Bless us, O Lord, and these your gifts,
> which we are about to receive
> from your bounty
> through Christ, our Lord.
> Amen.

> Gracious Giver of all good,
> we thank you for rest and food.
> Grant that all we do and say
> may serve you joyfully today.

Two favorite prayers of children are:

> God is great; God is good.
> Let us thank him for our food.

> Thank you for the world so sweet.
> Thank you for the food we eat.
> Thank you for the birds that sing.
> Thank you, God, for everything!

Scripture references also make wonderful prayers:

> Give thanks to the LORD, for he is good; his love endures forever.
> —Psalm 107:1

> Teach me to do your will, for you are my God; may your good Spirit lead me on level ground.
> —Psalm 143:10

Whether you speak grace out loud, sing it, or say it silently, always do so with a thankful heart.

People were saying that the coming winter would be long and hard. Mr. Miller claimed he could tell by looking at the woolly bear caterpillar's fuzz. "Too much black and not enough orange."

Mrs. Oates noticed, "Squirrels are gathering nuts early."

Mr. Hodge said, "Robins flew south ahead of time. We're in for a harsh season."

"Mama," Grace worried, "do you think our neighbors are right about the winter?" Harsh. The very word sounded like the hissing wind.

"Only God knows," Mama answered as she rocked baby Faith. "We have firewood stacked and food stored. Stop fretting and say a prayer instead. Now why don't you and Isaiah go down to the creek and ladle me a bucket of water for the stew?"

"Yes, Mama." Grace and her younger brother swished through the fallen leaves and breathed their delicious smell. Grace spun in circles under the still-warm sunshine. "What a glorious golden day, Isaiah!" she shouted, her worries forgotten for the moment.

Isaiah paid no attention. He was watching a box turtle munch a leaf.

When soaking rains came, going to school was impossible. "Unless you build an ark," Papa joked. Mama drilled Grace on her lessons until the puddles vanished.

Grace was happy as she once again made her way to school and met up with Hannah along the way. Hannah and Grace were both eight, best friends, and in third level.

It was a chilly morning, and Grace shivered as she and Hannah took their seats near the woodstove. Grace was glad for Mama's tutoring. She received a gold star for spelling that very afternoon!

On the way home, white fluffy flakes began falling.
"Hurrah!" yelled Hannah. "Here comes winter."
"Hurrah?" said Grace. "Winter frightens me."
"That's because you're a fretter, Grace," said Hannah,
waving good-bye when she reached her house.

Grace remembered last winter. Seven people had died from pneumonia, including Granny. In February, Papa went missing, stranded in a blizzard after going into town.

While he was gone, Mama birthed Faith way too soon. The baby was tiny and limp like a rag doll, and she'd whimpered like a kitten. Grace did Mama's chores as best she could. But even with the hard work, flaming hearth, and down-filled quilts, Grace always had been chilled.

In March, just as the creamy snowdrop flowers burst bravely through the softening soil, Papa returned, and Faith had cooed and wailed like a healthy baby. Mama praised God for his mercy.

No, Grace did not want another winter like last year's.

Grace went to her room and opened the Bible to the Psalms as her father taught her to do. The passage under her finger said that God takes good care of the birds, even though they do not reap or sow, and that he takes even better care of his children. "Please send us a gentle winter," Grace prayed.

Grace's prayer was answered. She waited for blizzards, but any snow that fell melted just as quickly. Grace recalled Mama's words:

Springtime passed, and by summer Faith was running and laughing. Isaiah's limbs outgrew his shirtsleeves and pants. Mama kept busy sewing, and Grace kept busy in the garden. She prayed for the right mix of rain and sun to grow the crops.

When harvest time came, everyone helped with the picking, plucking, heaving, hauling, peeling, cooking, canning, and storing.

Mrs. Oates's son Benjamin brought back a wife named Abigail, who told about a custom that had started in her settlement: Once a year everyone came together from miles around to share a harvest feast. Grace's neighbors liked that idea and set a date for their own fall celebration.

Grace and Hannah said, "We'll bake pies!"
For several days, they mashed pumpkin
flesh, boiled rhubarb stalks, and rolled
dough. They let Isaiah sprinkle apple slices
with sugar and cinnamon, and giggled when
he announced, "I'm the official taster."

Papa and Mr. Lambert made long wooden tables and benches. Mama and the other women stuffed pheasants and turkeys that the men and boys had hunted. The older girls minded the little ones while their parents worked.

When Grace and Hannah went to get water, Grace pointed to a squirrel holding a nut in its front paws. "It looks like it's praying, doesn't it?" she said.

As the girls scooped the sparkling water, Grace noticed four gulls circling. "It looks like they're singing praises to God," said Grace.

On the day of the fall feast, there were green salads, orange yams wrapped in cornhusks, ears of golden corn steaming in iron kettles, roasted meats, and fruity pies.

When everyone was seated, Papa said, "Let the feast begin!"

Spoons and platters clinked, and there was a hum of happy voices. Grace remembered the squirrel and the gulls. "Wait!" she shouted.

Everyone stopped and stared.

"Shouldn't we first say thank you to God and ask a blessing?"

"What an excellent idea, Grace," said Mr. Miller. "Why don't you say the prayer?"

Grace's mind raced. What would she say? What was that spelling word that meant "great generosity in giving"? She squeezed her eyes shut, and it came to her. Bounty. That was it!

As steamy aromas wafted up from the food, Grace gulped and raised her face to the sky. "Dear God in heaven," she said, "we thank you for your bounty. Please bless us and all our food. Amen."

"Amen!" the gathering echoed.

Noise began anew as plates and spirits overflowed.
Later with full bellies and thankful hearts, the adults talked
while the children played chase and invented new games.

The next morning when Grace's family sat down to breakfast,
Isaiah looked at his sister and said, "Say it, Grace."
Little Faith copied him. "Say Gwace!"

From that day forward, at every meal the family took turns "saying grace." Mama often quoted verses from the Bible. Papa talked to God as if he were an old friend, seated right there with them. Isaiah sang church songs, and Faith babbled away.

Grace wrote several new prayer-poems of her own. Sometimes she used words like bounty and giving. But she never, ever forgot the thanks.